KV-144-445

Ladybird books are widely available, but in case of difficulty may be ordered by post or telephone from:
Ladybird Books – Cash Sales Department Littlegate Road Paignton Devon TQ3 3BE Telephone 0803 554761

A catalogue record for this book is available from the British Library

Published by Ladybird Books Ltd Loughborough Leicestershire UK
LADYBIRD and the device of a Ladybird are trademarks of Ladybird Books Ltd

Printed in EC

Disney
Lady and the
TRAMP

Ladybird

One Christmas Eve, a small town was covered by a soft, white blanket of snow. Sleigh bells jingled in the crisp night air, and lights shone warmly from the houses. Inside, people were busy decorating trees and wrapping up presents.

When Christmas morning arrived, a tiny cocker spaniel puppy, wearing a big red ribbon, was placed in a hat box. She was very excited and couldn't wait to see what was going to happen next. Suddenly everything went quiet.

Then the puppy heard a door opening and two people approaching. As someone lifted her box, she recognized the voice of the man she had met in the pet shop.

"It's for you, Darling," the puppy heard him say. "Merry Christmas!"

"Oh, Jim Dear!" said his wife, starting to open the hat box. "It's the one I was admiring, isn't it, the one trimmed with ribbons?"

"Well," he replied, "it does have a ribbon!"

"How sweet!" cried Darling, as she picked up the puppy. "What a perfectly beautiful little lady!"

And that was how Lady got her name.

Lady loved her new home. Although they tried to make her sleep in her own basket in the kitchen, she preferred to snuggle down on Jim Dear and Darling's bed.

In the mornings, Lady chased the blackbirds in the garden, or buried her bones in the flowerbed. She frightened the rats in the woodpile, and *always* brought Jim Dear his morning paper. Everything was perfect.

When Lady was six months old, Darling gave her a smart blue collar. Lady looked at herself in the mirror. "It does look nice," she thought. "Won't Jock and Trusty be surprised!"

Jock, a small, black Scottish terrier, and Trusty, a big, brown bloodhound, were Lady's best friends. She set off to find them.

"Why, lassie, you've got a bonny new collar," said Jock admiringly. "It looks expensive! Have you shown it to Trusty yet?"

They found Trusty fast asleep on his porch. "Why, Miss Lady," he said, when at last he woke up and saw his friends, "you have a collar!"

"Yes, *and* a licence!" answered Lady proudly.

"That's the greatest honour man can bestow," said Trusty. "The badge of faith and respectability."

Lady was sure she was the most important member of Jim Dear and Darling's household. But one day, Lady realized that something was different. Jim Dear hadn't noticed her when she ran to meet him.

Then, a few weeks later, Darling stopped their afternoon walks together. Darling now spent all her time knitting, and she had even smacked Lady for playing with a ball of wool.

Lady lay down miserably beside her bowl and let the birds peck at her food.

"Why, lassie, is something wrong?" asked Jock. "Has somebody been mistreating you?"

"Oh, no, Jock!" she sighed. "It must be something *I've* done." She told her friends everything that had happened.

"Now, lassie, I wouldna worry," said Jock. "It's just that Darling is expecting a wee bairn."

"A bairn?" said Lady.

"He means a baby, Miss Lady," explained Trusty.

Lady still looked puzzled. "What's a baby?"

"Well, they're very like humans," said Trusty, "but smaller and sweeter. In fact, a baby is a cute little bundle of…"

"…trouble!" interrupted an unfamiliar voice behind them.

Lady turned in surprise to see a scruffy mongrel peeping round the gate. "Who are you?" she asked.

"Tramp's the name!" the stranger replied. "Remember this, Pigeon. A human heart has only so much room for love and affection. When a baby moves in, the dog moves out – to a leaky kennel."

The months passed, and winter gave way to spring. Many people came to visit Jim Dear and Darling, but no one paid any attention to Lady.

Then one evening in April a doctor arrived, and Jim Dear started acting very strangely. He ran up and down the stairs, shouting happily, “It’s a boy! Oh boy! A boy!”

Lady was puzzled and sad. “A baby must be something very wonderful,” she thought. “I must find out what it is.”

She crept silently up to the bedroom and watched Darling gently rocking a tiny white bundle in her arms, as she sang a lullaby. Lady went closer and Jim Dear lifted her up to see. Lady wagged her tail and smiled at the baby.

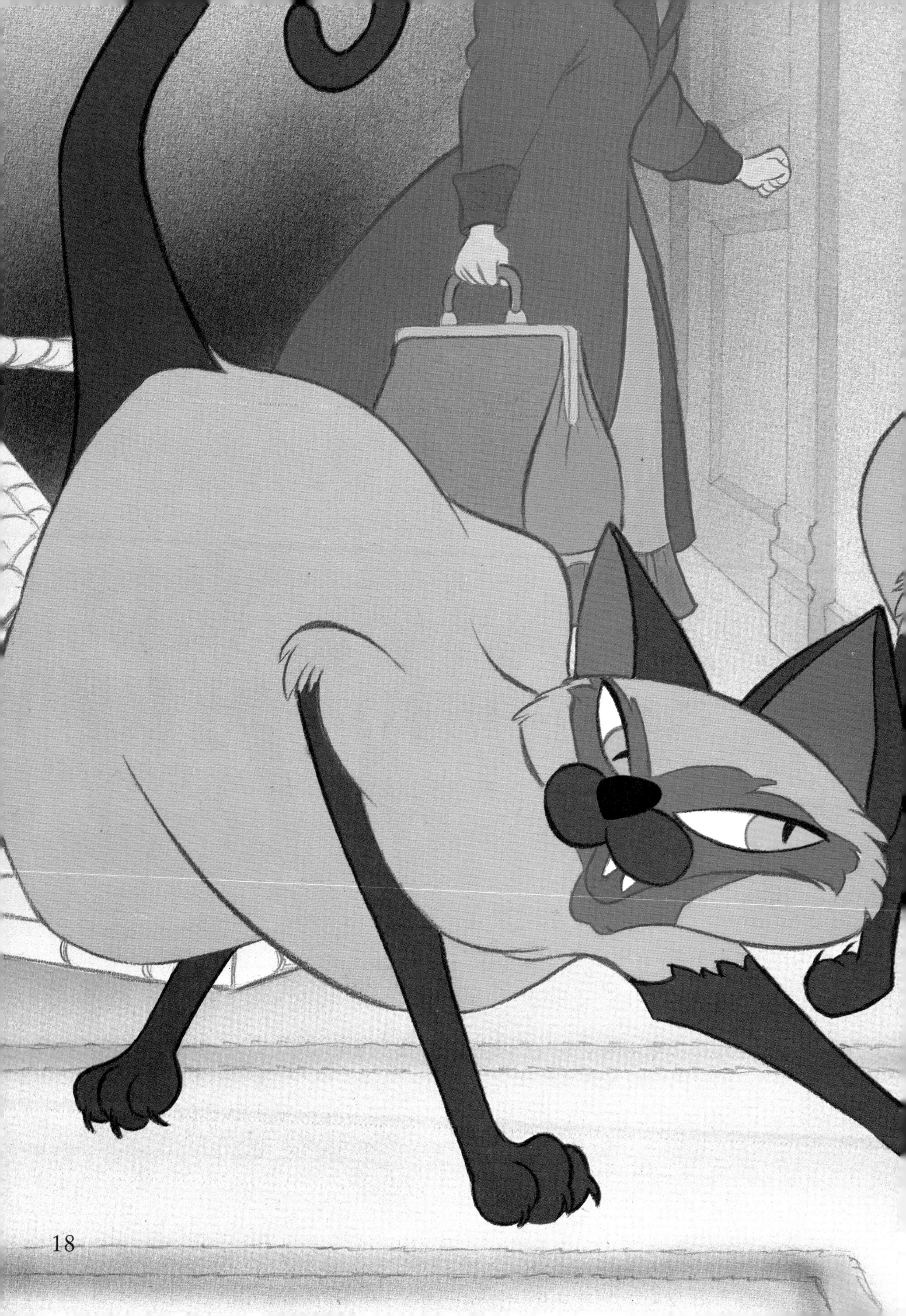

Sometime later Jim Dear and Darling went away for a few days. Lady had to stay behind, and someone called Aunt Sarah came to look after the baby.

Lady tried to lead the way to the nursery, but Aunt Sarah just shooed her back downstairs.

Looking sadly round the hall, Lady noticed two pairs of blue eyes peering out of Aunt Sarah's basket. Then two tails appeared. Suddenly, out popped two Siamese cats, who stalked menacingly up to Lady and hissed loudly.

Lady looked horrified and watched them creep past her towards the living room.

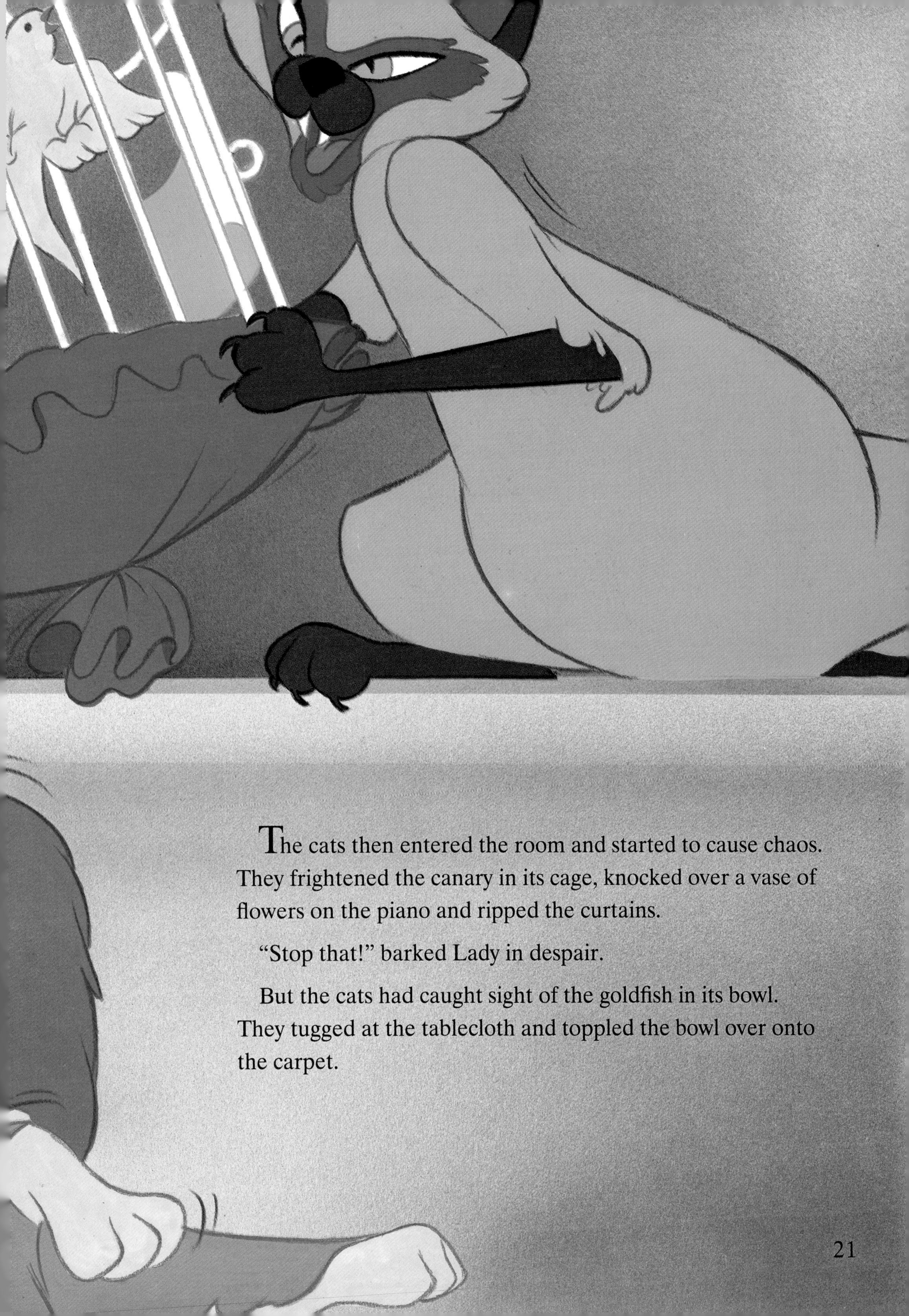

The cats then entered the room and started to cause chaos. They frightened the canary in its cage, knocked over a vase of flowers on the piano and ripped the curtains.

"Stop that!" barked Lady in despair.

But the cats had caught sight of the goldfish in its bowl. They tugged at the tablecloth and toppled the bowl over onto the carpet.

The cats tried to grab the goldfish, but fortunately Lady got there first. She gently picked up the poor fish and popped it back in its bowl.

Aunt Sarah, who had heard all the noise, came storming downstairs and into the room. The cats hid at once behind a chair, miaowing and pretending to be frightened.

"What's going on here?" she cried, when she saw the cats. "Oh, my darlings! My precious pets! You wicked dog, attacking my poor little angels."

So that very afternoon, Aunt Sarah took Lady to the pet shop. "I want a good, strong muzzle," she said.

"Ah, yes, ma'am," said the assistant. "Here's our latest combination muzzle and lead. Now, nice little doggie, we'll just slip it on like this."

Lady struggled wildly as they fastened the muzzle over her head. She leapt off the counter and made a dash for the door.

"Come back here!" cried Aunt Sarah. But Lady ran on and on.

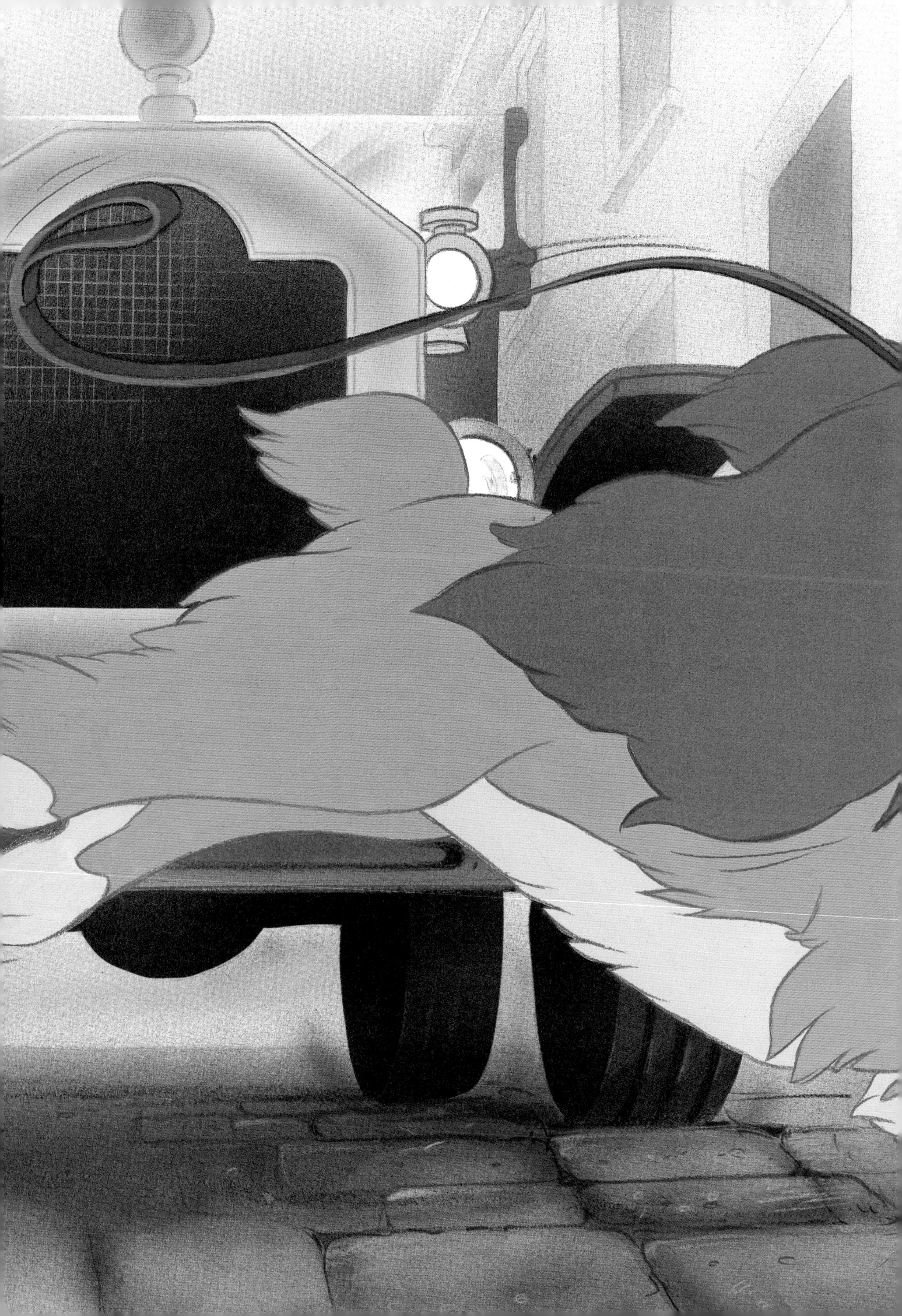

Poor Lady! She was so desperate to get away that she raced across the road and was nearly knocked down by a car. Her lead trailing behind her, she ran into a side road.

Suddenly a pack of stray dogs started to chase her. The muzzle slowed Lady down and made her an easy target.

Now it just so happened that Tramp was enjoying a quiet meal nearby. When he heard the sound of the dogs barking, he looked up and caught sight of Lady. Without a moment's delay, Tramp raced to the rescue. He knew all the streets and alleyways, and took a shortcut to catch up with the pack.

Baring his teeth and snarling in rage, Tramp leapt over the fence and faced Lady's attackers.

The dogs fought fiercely, but they were no match for this scruffy mongrel. He soon got the better of them and chased them away down the alley.

Tramp strolled back to Lady, who was still cowering in fear. “Hey, Pidge,” he said, “what are you doing here? I thought you lived…” Then he spotted the muzzle. “Hey, what’s this?” he asked.

Poor Lady couldn't say a word.

"You poor kid," said Tramp softly. "We've got to get that off. Hmmm… I think I know the very place. Come on!"

Tramp picked up Lady's lead in his mouth, and together they set off down the road.

To Lady's surprise, Tramp led her to the zoo.

They stopped outside the alligator's pool. The alligator was quite willing to assist, but Tramp didn't like the gleam in its eyes. He thought the alligator looked more hungry than helpful!

Tramp and Lady continued through the zoo looking for someone else to help them.

Soon they spotted a beaver who was hard at work, cutting up logs to build a dam. They persuaded the beaver to use his strong, sharp teeth to gnaw through the muzzle. At last, Lady was free.

"Come on, Pidge," said Tramp, when he had thanked the beaver, "let's find something to eat!" He led Lady through the streets to the back door of an Italian restaurant, and started to bark loudly.

"I'm-a coming!" called Tony, the restaurant owner, as he appeared in the doorway.

Tramp jumped up and licked him. "Hey, Joe!" shouted Tony to his waiter. "Bring me-a some bones for Butch-a before he eats-a me up!"

Then he saw Lady. "Hey, Joe! Look-a Butch-a. He-sa got a new girl friend!"

Tony brought out a table. "Hey, Joe, Butch-a he says he wants two spaghetti specials, heavy on the meatballs."

Lady looked at Tramp and smiled. Then they both tucked hungrily into their meal. Tony and Joe played soft, romantic music in the background.

"Oh, this is a beautiful night!" thought Lady, as she gazed up at the sky. Then she dreamily picked up another strand of spaghetti, and began to chew. Suddenly her lips met Tramp's. They were both eating the same strand of spaghetti!

After dinner, Tramp took Lady for a stroll in the park. The moon shone brightly as they put their paw prints next to each other's in some wet cement. Later the two dogs fell asleep under the stars.

The next morning, Lady woke with a start. "Oh dear!" she said. "I should have been home hours ago!"

"Why?" asked Tramp. "There is so much adventure and excitement in this great big world. It's ours, Pigeon!"

"But I must go back to look after the baby!" said Lady. So, shaking his head, Tramp agreed to take her home.

On the way, Tramp stopped suddenly. "Ever chase chickens?" he asked.

"I should say not!" said Lady, shocked.

"Ho, ho! Then you've never lived. Come on!" laughed Tramp, digging his way under the fence.

Lady followed as Tramp crept up to the hen house. He chased out the chickens, scampering after them with glee. Lady watched in horror, as feathers flew everywhere.

"Hey! What's going on?" came an angry voice. Suddenly bullets kicked up the dust in front of the dogs.

"That's the signal to get going!" said Tramp, racing round the corner. Lady ran after him, but she was soon left behind. A few minutes later, she was caught in a net. Before she knew what was happening, Lady was locked in a wagon and on her way to the dog pound.

"Put her in number four, Bill, while I check her licence number," said the guard at the pound.

Lady's eyes filled with tears as the door of her cell clanged shut behind her.

"Well, well. Look who's here. It's Miss Park Avenue herself!" jeered a large bulldog. "What are you in for, sweetheart? Putting fleas on the butler?"

"All right!" said Peg, a pretty little Pekingese. "Leave her alone, will you? Can't you see the poor kid's scared enough already?"

The other dogs quietened down. "They don't mean any harm really," said Peg, smiling at Lady. "And anyway, you'll be all right. Your licence is your passport to freedom, honey!"

Peg was right. It wasn't long before a guard came to fetch Lady – she was going home!

But Lady had spent enough time in the dog pound to learn several things about her new friend Tramp.

"He adores the ladies," Peg had said, "and they adore him. He breaks a new heart *every* day!"

It seemed that all the dogs in the pound knew everything about Tramp's adventures in the great big world.

Lady had thought that Tramp was special. But now she realized that he was just a scoundrel after all. She would try to forget him.

Back home, Aunt Sarah chained Lady up beside a kennel. Late that afternoon Jock and Trusty came to visit her.

"Please," said Lady sadly, "I don't want to see anybody."

"Now, now, lassie, don't feel like that," said Jock, and he tried to cheer her up.

As they were talking, Tramp trotted past the gate.

"Oh, Pigeon," he called.

"Humph!" said Lady, turning angrily away.

Jock and Trusty realized it was time for them to leave.

"Looks like I'm the one in the dog house," muttered Tramp. "It wasn't my fault," he pleaded. "I thought you were right behind me, honest! And when I heard they'd taken you to the dog pound..."

"Don't even mention that horrible place," Lady sobbed. "I was so frightened."

“And another thing,” Lady went on. “What about all the other ladies you’ve taken out to dinner – and all the hearts you’ve broken?” Tramp looked bewildered.

“I don’t need someone like you to shelter and protect me,” Lady cried. “I don’t even care if you get picked up by the dog catcher. Goodbye!” She turned and walked proudly into her kennel.

Tramp slunk away, wondering how he could put things right.

Lady leaned her head sadly over the edge of her kennel. A large tear rolled down her cheek. She watched the sky getting darker. She was sure there would be a storm.

As the thunder started to rumble, a large black rat peeped out of the woodpile, its red eyes gleaming. It scurried past Lady's kennel and ran towards the house.

Barking and growling fiercely, Lady tried to rush after the rat, but she was stopped by her chain.

The rat scampered up the flower trellis and jumped onto the roof. Lady struggled and struggled. It was no use – the chain held fast, and she watched the rat slip in through the nursery window.

Tramp heard Lady's frantic barking and came running back to see what was happening.

"What's wrong, Pidge?" he asked anxiously.

"A rat," she gasped, tugging hard at her chain. "Upstairs in the baby's room. Hurry! You can get in through the little door on the porch."

Tramp slipped into the house and up the stairs.

It was dark inside the nursery, but he could see the rat's eyes gleaming at the foot of the cot. He leapt towards it, snarling furiously.

The rat turned, and a fierce fight began.

Fur flew and teeth flashed as the two animals chased wildly round the room.

Meanwhile, Lady had managed to break her chain. She raced upstairs to help Tramp and reached the nursery just in time to see the rat jump onto the cot. Tramp leapt after it, knocking the cot over. Lady rushed forward to protect the baby.

The rat darted behind the curtains, but this time there was no escape – it was trapped. Tramp emerged victorious.

Lady looked at the dead rat in horror. Then she turned to Tramp, who was licking his wounds. Lady smiled at him. He had saved the baby – Tramp was forgiven.

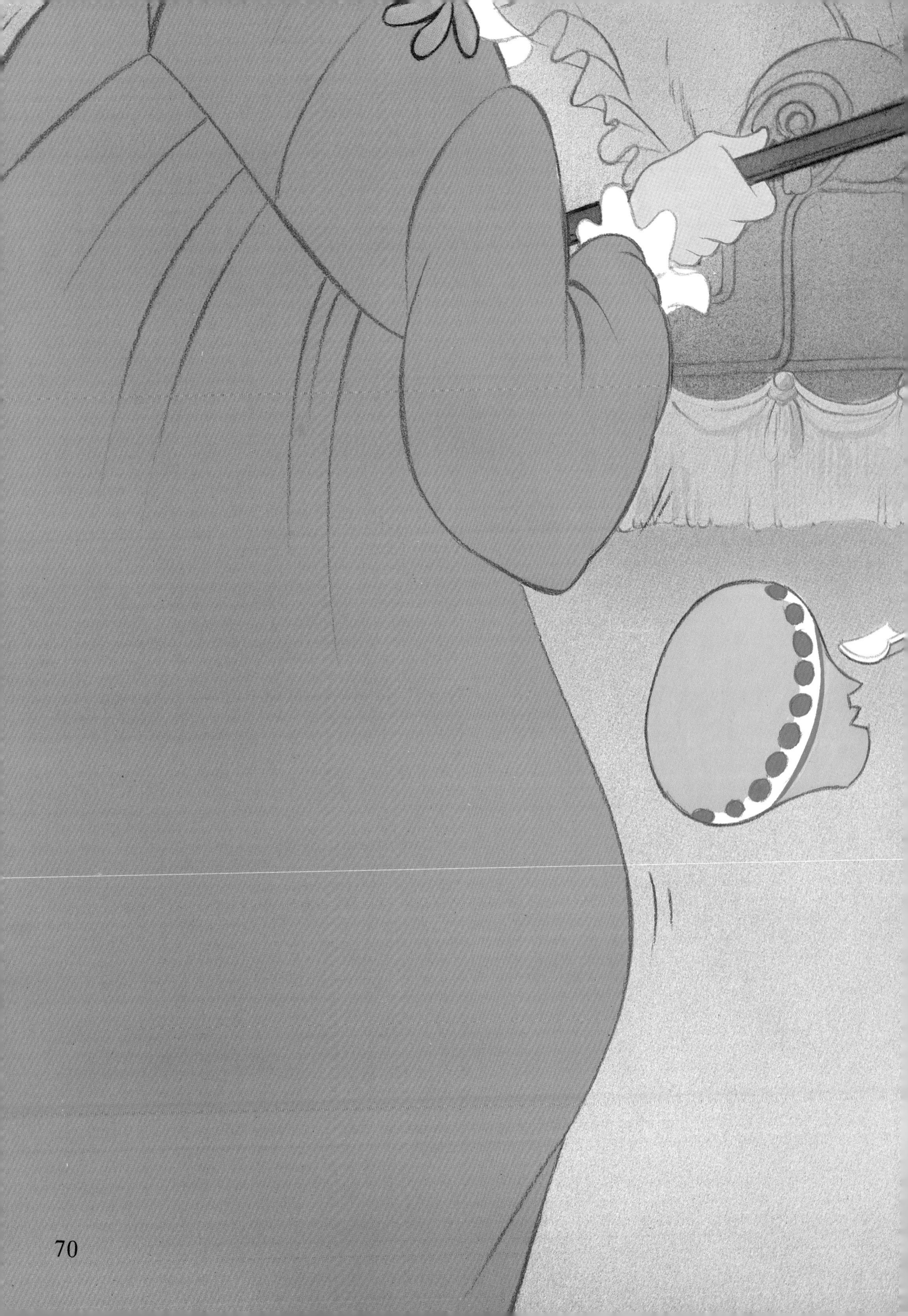

All the noise had wakened Aunt Sarah. She stormed into the room and found Lady and the Tramp standing beside the fallen cot.

"You poor little darling," she cried, picking up the baby. "Thank goodness you're not hurt." Then she looked at the two dogs. "You vicious brutes!" she shouted. "Get back! Go on! Get back!" Aunt Sarah grabbed a broom, pushed Tramp into a cupboard and locked the door.

Aunt Sarah dragged Lady downstairs. "Come on!" she cried. "I'll call the dog pound this minute. I won't sleep a wink with that brute in the house."

Lady was thrust into the cellar. She heard Aunt Sarah pick up the telephone and order the dog catcher to take Tramp away.

Not long afterwards, the dog catcher arrived and put Tramp into the wagon. As he was about to drive away, Jim Dear and Darling came home. "What's going on here?" asked Jim Dear.

"Just picking up a stray dog, mister," said the dog catcher, moving his horses forward. "Caught him attacking a baby!"

Jock and Trusty heard every word. They knew that Tramp was a mongrel, but they couldn't believe he would do anything like that. "We've got to try to help him!" said Trusty.

As soon as Lady heard Jim Dear's voice, she started to bark and scratch at the cellar door.

"I'm sure there must be some mistake," said Jim Dear, as he opened the door. "I know that Lady wouldn't..."

Lady rushed out, barking with excitement, and ran up the stairs.

"Watch out!" said Aunt Sarah. "That dog's loose! Keep her away!"

"Nonsense!" said Jim Dear. "She's trying to tell us something," and he followed Lady up the stairs.

"What is it, old girl?" asked Jim Dear as they entered the nursery. Lady hurried over to the curtains. Jim Dear went across and lifted them up. "Darling! Aunt Sarah! Come here!" he called.

"Oh, how horrible. A dead rat!" squealed Aunt Sarah.

Jim Dear realized instantly that it was Tramp who had killed the rat and had saved his baby's life.

Taking Lady with him, Jim Dear rushed out of the house and stopped a passing taxi. They jumped inside and Jim Dear told the driver to head for the dog pound as quickly as he could.

In the meantime, Trusty was carefully following the scent of the wagon, with Jock close at his heels. When they caught up with it, Trusty raced ahead of the horses. They reared up in fright.

"Whoa there!" cried the dog catcher in alarm. "Get away!"

There was nothing he could do. His wagon tipped over onto its side.

When Jim Dear's taxi skidded to a halt behind the toppled wagon, Lady jumped out and ran to the back. She was overjoyed to find Tramp unhurt.

But Trusty was trapped under one of the broken wheels. Jock ran to his side and kept nudging him, but his faithful friend did not stir. Jock howled in despair.

Some time later, two visitors arrived at the home of Jim Dear and Darling. Lady and the Tramp rushed downstairs to greet them. There was Jock–*and* Trusty! The bloodhound had survived the accident but he had broken his leg. He limped slowly down the snowy path.

"Why, you've got a collar!" said Trusty. "And a licence!"

"Yep!" said Tramp, grinning proudly.

"And how do you like your new home?" asked Jock.

"Well," said Tramp, looking cheekily at Lady, "after all my adventures in the great big world… it is nice to have a *proper* home at last."

Christmas Eve came again. But this time, there were four little puppies under the Christmas tree. Three of them were as beautiful as Lady, and the fourth looked just like Tramp. He was every bit as mischievous as his father…

…and every bit as lovable!